Sony Pictures
Animation

SMURFS™
THE LOST VILLAGE

Smurfette
and the Lost Village

Adapted by Daphne Pendergrass
Illustrated by Antonello Dalena   Colors by Paolo Maddaleni

Simon Spotlight
New York   London   Toronto   Sydney   New Delhi

SIMON SPOTLIGHT
An imprint of Simon & Schuster Children's Publishing Division
1230 Avenue of the Americas, New York, New York 10020
This Simon Spotlight edition February 2017
SMURFS™ & © Peyo 2017 Licensed through Lafig Belgium/IMPS. Smurfs: The Lost Village, the Movie © 2017
Columbia Pictures Industries, Inc. and LSC Film Corporation. All Rights Reserved.
SIMON SPOTLIGHT and colophon are registered trademarks of Simon & Schuster, Inc.
For information about special discounts for bulk purchases, please contact Simon & Schuster Special Sales at 1-866-506-1949 or business@simonandschuster.com.
Manufactured in the United States of America 0217 LAK
2 4 6 8 10 9 7 5 3
ISBN 978-1-4814-8055-0
ISBN 978-1-4814-8056-7 (eBook)

It was a beautiful day in Smurf Village, but Smurfette was sad. She wanted to have Smurfy purpose like the other Smurfs. Hefty Smurf was strongest, Brainy Smurf was smartest, and Clumsy Smurf was, well, clumsiest!

Smurfette was different. The evil wizard Gargamel had originally created her from a block of clay. He wanted Smurfette to be evil, but Papa Smurf had helped her become good. Ever since, Smurfette had wondered: What was she best at? What was *her* purpose?

Later that day Brainy was testing a new invention called the Smurfy Thing Finder th[...]
could reveal what each Smurf did best. The invention seemed to be working. It had sai[...]
Hefty was strong!

"Maybe your machine can smurf me what I'm best at," Smurfette said to Brainy, but [...]
when she tried to use the machine, it broke! Somehow Smurfette took the energy out o[...]
it! Now she felt bad for breaking Brainy's invention *and* for not having a purpose!

Hefty had an idea to cheer her up—Smurf-boarding! Soon Smurfette, Hefty, Brainy, and Clumsy were zooming around the woods outside Smurf Village on Smurf-boards. "Woo-hoo!" Smurfette cheered as she flew over them all, toward the Forbidden Forest, a magical place that Papa did not allow them to enter. When she landed, though, she looked up and gasped—it was a Smurf she'd never seen before! The Smurf ran away into the forest, but left a hat behind. Smurfette picked it up and stared at it in wonder.

Suddenly Gargamel's vulture, Monty, swooped in, grabbed Smurfette, and brought her back to Gargamel's lair. Gargamel wanted to steal her smurfy magic, but was disappointed because she wasn't a real Smurf! When he saw that Smurfette was carryin a little hat, though, he tossed it into his cauldron. The cauldron bubbled and said, "Th hat is from a village of Smurfs," and showed an image of three tall trees.

"A new Smurf village? I will catch those Smurfs too, and take their Smurfy magic!" Gargamel cackled.

While he was distracted, Smurfette's friends were able to break in and free her!

When she returned to Smurf Village, Smurfette was determined to save the mysterious smurfs. She decided to set out into the Forbidden Forest to find their village. While sneaking out, she ran into Hefty, Brainy, and Clumsy.

"I have to do this," Smurfette said before they could try to stop her. "If there really is a lost village of Smurfs, they need help. Maybe *that's* my purpose!"

"Yeah, well, Team Smurf sticks together, so we're going with you," Hefty said.

The four friends entered the Forbidden Forest, but they soon realized there was a big problem in their way: Gargamel was determined to get to the lost village first!

"All right, boys," Gargamel called to Monty and his cat, Azrael. "Catch those Smurfs!"

"In here!" Smurfette called to her friends, and they quickly hid in rabbit holes.

Inside, there were tunnels with magical creatures—Glow-Bunnies! The bunnies were very friendly, and they swept the Smurfs up onto their backs.

The Smurfs rode the Glow-Bunnies as they stampeded out of the tunnels, escaping from Gargamel to continue on their journey.

It wasn't long before Smurfette saw a familiar sight. "I think those are the three tall trees I saw in Gargamel's cauldron!"

The trees were on the other side of an enchanted river.

"Fear not, Team Smurf!" Brainy said.

Brainy quickly built a raft! The Smurfs hopped on, waved good-bye to the Glow-Bunnies, and sailed off.

Their peaceful river ride quickly turned rocky. Team Smurf rushed to steer the raft way from Gargamel, who was just downstream, floating on a log!

Wham! Gargamel's log collided with a boulder, and he fell into the river. "Help! lease! I can't swim!" he said, thrashing about in the water. He really did look like he as in trouble.

"We gotta help," Hefty said.

Brainy and Clumsy were surprised that Hefty wanted to help Gargamel, their enemy!

"I hate Gargamel more than anyone, but we're Smurfs," Smurfette told them. "We smurf the right thing." With that, Hefty steered the raft back to Gargamel. Gargamel knocked the Smurfs into the water, and they tumbled over a waterfall!

Team Smurf swam to the riverbank, wet but unharmed. Before they had time to catch
their breath, arrows rained down on them! A group of strange, masked creatures herded
the Smurfs into the woods and stopped when they arrived at a grassy grove.
"Who are you? What do you want?" Hefty asked the creatures.
One of them removed its mask, revealing . . .

A girl Smurf! "I'm Smurfwillow!" she said. "I'm the leader, and these are my friends, Smurfblossom and Smurfstorm."

The creatures began taking off their masks—they were all girl Smurfs!

"Where are all your boys?" Smurfette asked.

"You won't find any boys here," said Smurfwillow. "Welcome to Smurfy Grove. A villa one hundred girls strong."

Smurfette was in shock, but there wasn't time for chitchat.

"We came to warn you about the evil wizard Gargamel," Smurfette said to
Smurfwillow.

Smurfwillow wasn't worried. The three tall trees that marked the village weren't
trees at all; they were the waterfalls that Team Smurf had fallen in. And the trees
that Gargamel had sailed toward were actually part of the Swamp of No Return! Still,
Smurfstorm and Clumsy went to the swamp to make sure Gargamel was gone for good.
They rode on the back of a Dragonfly!

Meanwhile, Smurfette, Hefty, and Brainy took a tour of Smurfy Grove. It was beautifu
Unlike the Smurfs in Smurf Village, the Smurfy Grove girls didn't do just one thing: Each
Smurf was strong *and* smart *and* kind *and* creative *and* more!

Hefty and Brainy had fun trying new things. They even sewed quilts!

Smurfette was in awe. She flew in the air using flower petals, painted, took archery
lessons, and zipped around on leaves pulled by bees! Smurfette smiled . . . but then
ere was a commotion outside.

Suddenly, Smurfstorm and Clumsy returned from the swamp with bad news.

"They were right!" Smurfstorm told Smurfwillow. "Gargamel is on his way! And Smurfette led him right to us!"

Her words hit Smurfette like a ton of bricks. In a way she *had* led Gargamel to Smurf Grove, even if it wasn't on purpose.

"Smurfette came to *help* you!" Hefty shouted back.

As the Smurfs started arguing, Papa Smurf showed up!
"You four Smurfs are coming home with me right now," he said. He was angry at Smurfette and the others for leaving home. Then Smurfette explained that Gargamel was nearby, and Papa became worried. "We've got to clear out of here before Gargamel finds—" *Boom!* Before he could finish his sentence, Papa and Smurfwillow were hit with Gargamel's freeze spells! There were more flashes as Gargamel froze more of the villagers, along with Hefty, Brainy, and Clumsy.

"Prepare for Garmageddon!" Gargamel cackled, towering over the Smurfs. Then the evil wizard began scooping them up into a bag to take back to his lair.

"Smurfette, how could you do this to us?" Smurfblossom said between tears.

"Because it's her *purpose*," Gargamel answered with a laugh. Then he left Smurfy Grove with all of the frozen Smurfs in tow.

Alone in the forest, Smurfette cried and cried. Could it be true? Had she really betrayed her friends?

As she looked up, she saw Brainy's assistant, Snappy Bug, land beside her. Snappy reminded Smurfette of her great friends and that Smurfs always do the right thing. With renewed strength, Smurfette wiped away her tears and took off after Gargamel.

When Smurfette arrived at Gargamel's lair, the frozen Smurfs were back to normal, bu
Gargamel was trying to drain them of their magic. She had to act fast!

"Gargamel!" Smurfette called. "I've come to pledge my loyalty. Smurf your power
to turn me back into who I once was, and I'll lead you to Smurf Village. There are
ninety-five Smurfs waiting there now. Together, we'll be unstoppable."

Gargamel raised his arms and cast a magic spell. "Welcome home, Smurfette!"

Smurfette knew something that Gargamel didn't: She was a power magnet! Just as he'd sucked all the power from Brainy's invention, she absorbed the power and magic out of Gargamel and sent the evil wizard and his pets flying through the roof!

When the dust settled, the Smurfs saw that Gargamel's spell had changed Smurfette into her original form—a clay statue. They cried as they carried their hero back to Smurf Village.

"Smurfette had more good in her than all of us combined," Papa wept. "She never believed she was a real Smurf, but she was the *truest* Smurf of all."

As the Smurfs stood in a circle around Smurfette, the power of love—two hundred Smurfs strong—magically brought Smurfette back to life!

Smurfette was happy. In the lost village she found out she could have more than just *one* purpose: She was a friend, a leader, a dancer, a captain, a flower-glider, a bunny-wrangler, and most of all, a true-blue Smurf!